COSTUMES
OF THE LIVING

Gaurav Monga is the author of *Tears for Rahul Dutta* (Philistine Press, 2012), *Family Matters* (Eibonvale Press, 2019) and *Ruins* (Desirepaths Publishers, 2019). His work has appeared in diverse literary magazines, such as the *Fanzine, Tammy Journal, Queen Mobs Teahouse, Juked,* and *BODY* among others. He is originally from New Delhi, and teaches creative writing and German at schools and colleges.

gaurav monga

COSTUMES OF THE LIVING

THIS IS A SNUGGLY BOOK

ISBN: 978-1-64525-044-9

The cover shows photographs attributed to Jacques Lalaing, done c. 1883-1914, in the Rijksmuseum, Amsterdam.

In loving memory of Carla Aiello

Oft wenn ich Kleider mit vielfachen Falten, Rüschen und Behängen sehe, die über schönen Körper schön sich legen, dann denke ich, daß sie nicht lange so erhalten bleiben, sondern Falten bekommen, nicht mehr geradezuglätten, Staub bekommen, der, dick in der Verzierung, nicht mehr zu entfernen ist, und daß niemand so traurig und lächerlich sich wird machen wollen, täglich das gleiche kostbare Kleid früh anzulegen und abends auszuziehn.

Doch sehe ich Mädchen, die wohl schön sind und vielfach reizende Muskeln und Knöchelchen und gespannte Haut und Massen dünner Haare zeigen, und doch tagtäglich in diesem einen natürlichen Maskenanzug erscheinen, immer das gleiche Gesicht in die gleichen Handflächen legen und von ihrem Spiegel widerscheinen lassen.

Nur manchmal am Abend, wenn sie spät von einem Feste kommen, scheint es ihnen im Spiegel abgenützt, gedunsen, verstaubt, von allen schon gesehn und kaum mehr tragbar.

—Franz Kafka, *Kleider*

Often when I see clothes with manifold pleats, frills, and appendages which fit so smoothly onto lovely bodies I think they won't keep that smoothness long, but will get creases that can't be ironed out, dust lying so thick in the embroidery that it can't be brushed away, and that no one would want to be so unhappy and so foolish as to wear the same valuable gown every day from early morning till night.

And yet I see girls who are lovely enough and display attractive muscles and small bones and smooth skin and masses of delicate hair, and nonetheless appear day in, day out, in this same natural fancy dress, always propping the same face on the same palms and letting it be reflected from the looking glass.

Only sometimes at night, on coming home late from a party, it seems in the looking glass to be worn out, puffy, dusty, already seen by too many people, and hardly wearable any longer.

—Franz Kafka, *Clothes*

I must remember to write about my clothes next time I have an impulse to write. My love of clothes interests me profoundly; only is it not love; and what it is I must discover

—Virginia Woolf

COSTUMES OF THE LIVING

TRIBES AND CASTES

Only at the time of extreme grief of having lost a loved one, were we permitted to unleash our sorrow by tearing our clothes. If we lacked the strength to do so, we were permitted to use scissors, only if scissors were at our disposal at that given moment of grief; using them would not have been permitted even a moment later, should the grief have disappeared. Children, especially of the female sex, were, however, not encouraged to tear their own clothes even if they possessed the strength. A mere cut in the cloth, like that of a small blouse that was not visible to the public eye would have sufficed.

⌘

Because he had lost his father so young, he spent many of his growing-up years lonely, staring at his naked body in front of a mirror. The death of his father is what drove him to making clothes and taking photographs of himself. It was that early impulse that impelled him to cut—when he was dirt poor—his stiff white collars out of chart paper. He also made sure that he remained excessively thin and sometimes even starved himself.

⌘

Unlike other dresses of the time, some of which were cylindrical graves to house a corpse, this dress clung to the contours of her body, and all the folds and pleats, like the edges of her body, allowed for her clothes to be enjoyed as flesh.

⌘

It took only a single sharp cut with scissors to dispel all air of mystery. The cloth, lying crushed for many years in a cupboard, would in one fell swoop cease to remember. The only way to avoid this would be to either fold in the undesired cloth, rendering it invisible, or to soften the scissors by wrapping them in yarn.

⌘

Underneath her skin one found earrings made of gold, silver and even plastic. There were wigs, hair extensions, colored contact lenses, push-up bras underneath her skin.

⌘

The children who drowned in the lake that day left all their clothes piled up on a grassy patch.

⌘

As a young boy he had hated his sister so much that he spent one afternoon while she was away at ballet class cutting up her dresses with a small pair of scissors.

⌘

The dress was endless in its manifold pleats and creases, so much so that each fold led to another. It was as if each fold, gathering dust in its crevices, played its own part in remembering.

HOW TO DRESS

All the clothes that we would ever make would always be stitched from the ones we already owned, clothes that were either growing old, or had never been worn.

⌘

The woolen coat that he wore had been stripped of that lamb outside his apartment that he used to often see grazing in rugged fields.

⌘

During those war days we were always in each others' clothes and linens, for all the clothing stores had been raided and some even bombed.

⌘

The entire outfit was complex, as it was composed of various yarns and fabric of multiple colors, not to mention buttons, sashes and zips that kept it taut, all together. The entire outfit was complete in its multiply distinct parts, and apart from a hanging necktie—the sign of a dead man—each article of clothing played its necessary part in finishing off the whole dress, so much so that neither body nor mannequin was needed.

⌘

All those men who died young were buried in clothes befitting children.

⌘

The city has finally come into full-bloom, crowded with offices and people in suits. City fashion has even taken villages by storm, so much so that farmers have started wearing their suits into the fields.

SPECIAL ORNAMENTATION

With all this loose thread lying about, you can stitch up a whole person . . . . . .

At the depot, all clothing is taken away from prisoners on their arrival. In this prison you have not only convicts washing the uniforms of other convicts but of policeman and jailers, as well. Small wheelbarrows full of worn-out clothing can be seen at most times either being carted around the prison premises or merely standing still. The uniforms for policemen, convicts, jailers and even judges are stitched by convicts in a small room in the attic. Even the supreme court judge sends his servant there to retrieve his clothes. It would, as a result, be natural to assume that much of what transpires in this prison is being woven into the fabric of these dirty uniforms.

⌘

Because they introduced sweatshirts with hoods on them, the sales of winter caps plummeted rapidly, so much so that warehouses needed to dump these caps. But where would those clothes go? Would not all of that excessive fabric lie about on the surface of the earth uselessly and bother us if we were to think about those unworn caps?

⌘

Only in hindsight was he able to see that all that went wrong revolved essentially around what they wore, so much so that it could possibly be posited that there was no other real, at least tangible cause for their ruin. Her mother in law could not stand that her son's wife continued to wear his underwear. She even told her son that because of her even he had started to dress badly, which is why she decided to gift both of them new clothes, including dresses which her daughter in law didn't have much opportunity to wear, for she had confined herself to the house, garden and the dogs, and slowly he too didn't see much sense in gallivanting in the city by himself. Soon their wardrobe had only loose, worn-out clothing for the home, napkins, socks.

PLAIN AND COLORED

In this new religious following, the nuns and monks walked about all day in robes of different color and ornament, designating their position and function. Although this was a new religion, one born in our very own times, only the high priest — they were and could only be twelve—wore a robe that was different from everyone else's. The belief was that the men or possibly even women—we, most likely would never know—in these distinctively unique robes should always remain hidden, that only by virtue of their invisibility will the human race endure. It, as a result, goes without saying that the robes worn by these men or women will never be seen, unless of course by accident.

⌘

It all happened when he stepped out of those impeccably ironed Italian handmade suits into rags. Now, that he had taken to religion and charity giving, he left his expensive blue car with leather seats rotting in the parking space. Instead he walked everywhere wearing only hand-me-downs, refusing to buy new clothes. Even if someone had gifted them to him, he would have insisted on dirtying them right away.

⌘

Fashion magazines have had a posthumous revival even after we had stopped wearing clothes, altogether. For some reason, it didn't matter whether we had ever worn clothes at all. Often, however, just for fun, or for some aesthetic or haptic and perhaps sexual pleasure, a sole dress, or a pair of pants would be produced superfluously to comment and moreover remind people what clothing once must have really looked and felt like, for the fashion magazines had begun already a long time ago to produce something of an unimaginable nature.

⌘

The body of a clown, by virtue of a color scheme, seems symmetrical, but is in fact intentionally sewn out of joint, as the fabric on one side is a lot heavier than the other.

LOONGEES AND DHOTEES

In many countries, mass rituals to vent frustration involve the use of clothing. Unhappy with clean,dry clothes, people begin to wet their clothes, soaked in water and sometimes fresh dye, leaving often traces of color on the skin. Sometimes, the main incentive is to get rid of the cloth altogether by burning it till there is nothing left. People, however, who can't decide what to do with their clothes often leave with the charred remains.

COTTON BORDERS

When they arrested him, he was wearing an old nightshirt and underwear, while the policeman had on an elegant black robe with intricate, ornate gold handiwork, something he could not help but notice while he was being dragged away.

At the police station they made him strip while all the other policemen stared at this lonely body. His nightshirt and underwear were placed in a little basket and put aside. He was almost certain that his clothes would get mixed up with somebody else's.

It, nevertheless, appeared to him (only him) at that juncture that the prospective trial was in fact going to work in his favor, for the policeman, whilst interrogating him while he was still half asleep, somehow forgot about all the other dirty linen that must have been stacked away in his cupboard.

Whiling his time in prison like a dog who only needed to be whistled for to return to his cage, he never came across the policeman who had arrested him or for that matter any other policeman dressed in the same clothes. Perhaps, it was that policeman's sole task as a policeman to arrest no one but him.

Could he, however, not have been better prepared? He was now convinced that had he been wearing something else when the policeman had showed or if he had at least given him the chance to change into something else—he imagined carefully putting on his only black suit—his trial would have turned out differently.

⌘

My sister and I would take all our clothes to the lake and enter from a secret trail, as if the path, our march to the water was as important as the swim. Sometimes on the way, we would intentionally trade shorts. She would wear mine, and I, hers, as if I could be in her—my lost sister—and she could be in me in this secret fashion. But when our parents saw that we'd traded shorts, we would blush just like the little children we were.

⌘

In a tailor's shop, one could veritably become dizzy, staring at all that fabric, at all the pins and needles, and just the sheer variety of clothing articles: buttons, thread, torn off collars, not to mention the tailor's hands that spent a whole lifetime touching fabric between thick fingers.

⌘

This one piece suit didn't only trace the out-line of the wearer's form but also moved with her every movement so much so that each movement became ingrained in this article of clothing, in its memory.

This one piece suit of ivory hue could have well been likened to an ever-moving set of physical postures and gesticulations and at best could be thought of as sculpture in flux. At times, however, it would suddenly come to a complete standstill and get stuck in a single immutable tragic bow or strange side-ways movement of worn out cloth.

GAUZE-LIKE TEXTURE

With this dress there was not even one spot that was untouched. The suit was full proof and perfectly complete, leaving not even a single weak spot—an entryway— except for the chance possibility that the wearer would momentarily forget to button his sleeves.

⌘

Someday her scarf will choke her to death.

⌘

With all that tightly, slim-fitted clothing, even thin people gradually began to wear shirts and trousers fit for giants, as some sort of circus trick

⌘

Those days I liked to wear rags, not really but I somehow ended up wearing them anyway. I once went clothes shopping with my English teacher and picked up some real fancy clothes. I looked so different, so sophisticated. I like looking sophisticated, but I rarely do. It's because most fancy clothes don't fit me. My parents laugh at me when I wear sophisticated clothes. It is probably because I am too young to be wearing them. I don't feel young. Inside, I feel like a much older person. I even behave like it but my parents don't notice such small things. My English teacher once told me that I behave like an older person, and that is bad in one way, as children my age don't want to spend time with me, but good in another, as it will make sure that I won't do childish things.

⌘

My English Teacher once told me that the only reason she liked to dress so excessively—adorned with ornament—and liked to kiss me profusely in front of the other students was not because she didn't believe that she was a good teacher, but because, at bottom, she hated herself. Sometimes, instead of undressing, she donned twenty pairs of underwear and multiple bras, making it impossible to breathe.

⌘

Even later when I started wearing better clothes, I thought at the time that I put myself well out in the world by being well-dressed, and the truth was that I truly was. But now I realise how others must have looked at me in those clothes that were admittedly nice but not tailored well enough to fit me. My pants were always a little too tight and my shirts never quite fit my torso. It would have perhaps been far more respectable to have worn clothes that were never intended to look good, in the first place.

⌘

In the spring, she often arrives wearing a sweater that makes her look pregnant. On the waist it appears that she, herself, has stitched on two circular leather pads vaguely reminiscent of a womb.

⌘

If she were to write her own biography, it would be filled with endless dresses but unlike other dresses of the time, her dresses would be made to unfold in ways that would go against the folds of her flesh. A blemish or stain that surfaced on the cloth would emerge from some deeper inner wound, like acne on skin, and unlike all those starved torn jeans, those tight tubercular pink shirts most women her age wore, her flowing dresses hanging on the clothes-line would blow gently in the breeze.

⌘

She would always tell me that had it not have been for my confidence in her, she would have never started wearing sleeveless shirts to reveal her unusually fat arms. She had always felt ever since she was a teenage girl that there was something wrong with her body, for no matter what she wore, it never looked right. Perhaps, it was because she grew up looking at her obese aunts and even though later she grew exceedingly thin, she nevertheless insisted on leaving a T-shirt on while in a public swimming pool, supposedly in order to conceal her small teenage breasts from the stares of disgusting men, but be that as it may, her T-shirt continues to weigh her down, almost threatening to drown her.

MADRAS IS BLEACHED

The city in which I live in now has become polluted. We walk about town in circles, not noticing that over the years our clothes have accumulated so much dust that it has ruined our appearance.

⌘

She kept all her secrets—not to mention her money—hidden in her underwear. Even when she was homeless, she felt that when she wore her dresses, she was inside a house.

⌘

She would spend most of her days unemployed, idle and would worry about falling sick again. As a result, she started ironing her clothes obsessively, believing somewhere that there may well arrive a time when our clothes will replace our bodies, a time when by merely ironing out a crease on a blouse, one would be able to cure cancer of the breasts, or by a simple fold inhibit bacteria and other illnesses from spreading.

⌘

Sometimes, even I liked to dress her up, often in the tattered clothes I found lying about her house or sometimes even when we used to go shopping in the mall. I would choose her colors and fabric, and though we did not touch each other, the handing over of all those green and blue sweaters, white and mauve skirts in and out of the changing cabin from above the curtain, left some sort of trace of our hands upon the fabric.

Often, when the clothes did not fit, she used to confound the tailor working in the shop by arguing that in her special case it would not be the clothes that would be made to fit her body but rather parts of her body had to be trimmed and in some cases cut off, to make sure the clothes fit.

Her dresses were a trap that folded only inward. In fact, there was no window that looked out. One could never have really been certain whether they might have folded so far in as to render an unfolding body of the same cloth.

⌘

I once even asked her what her relationship with clothes was, to which she replied that ever since she began dressing up and had begun to notice her own body and clothes—especially in front of a mirror—she felt somehow she had come closer to dying.

⌘

With great desperation, I have tried to offer meaning to this remaining lump of yarn with which she would have churned out sweaters for her children and adorned their dolls with jackets and socks.

⌘

She gave away her clothes to her sister because they did not fit her anymore, as she had suddenly grown unexpectedly thin, which made her look a lot older. A few months later, she began gaining weight again and asked her sister to return her clothes. By then, it was already too late, for her sister had by now made in them a new home.

DACCA MUSLINS

He put on his clothes and finally felt that he could hide everything, even the large breasts that were hidden underneath the soft loose shirt, and even after he lost all that weight, his breasts remained. Often at night he would try and convince his wife to fondle them but underneath his clothes, whilst walking on the streets, he was someone else.

⌘

He had saved that shirt he wanted to wear under that brown sweater for a day that he would be with a well dressed woman or man;

he would have liked for her or him to notice the white collar against the brown woolen sweater.

⌘

Students wear the same dull uniform to school everyday.

⌘

He took it upon himself once he had sufficient funds, to always appear impeccably well dressed, even in his own living room. For him there was no difference between the suit he wore to work and after working hours with friends in a coffee shop. The only place where he would let go was in his own bed, amidst the cold, satin sheets, he would sleep naked.

⌘

This transsexual wore his false breasts, his slim supple effeminate body like a long permanent dress.

⌘

In order to enter the temple, you must first completely undress, and even then you may not be permitted.

CRIMSON MERINO

She suddenly stopped receiving his calls for reasons he could not grasp. Many months later, at a bus stop, not far from where they lived, he caught her red-handed with all his clothes on—his shirt, his pants and from the looks of it, even his socks had been stolen from his drawers.

⌘

The children who drowned in the lake that day left all their clothes piled up on a grassy patch.

⌘

Do you remember what clothes you were wearing when all this happened?

⌘

In a city where no one knows you and the women are all dead, you would like to walk out on to the streets in the most despicable and tasteless attire.

EN DRAPERIE

Even if my clothes are dirty, I know that all I need to do is take them off to be good again, because my body is fine, and now all that I need to do is to put some fresh clothes on.

⌘

This secret exchange of clothes took place only at night when most of us were asleep. We would hear a knock at the door, someone left a pile of soiled underwear. In fact, all over town one would find these soiled underwear outside people's front doors.

⌘

The clown was now just a bag of clothes, his body inside that costume had grown limp.

⌘

Already as a young child, he had developed his own sense of style in respect to his attire and was not just something his mother put haphazardly together.

NATIVE WEAVERS

Women started wearing furs when they first began shaving their pubic hair.

⌘

Both men and women were forced to wear clothes of a single color; they were allowed only to wear varying shades of blue. One woman got the tailor to stitch her a blue gown whose inner lining was bright orange. The joy she must have felt to roll up her sleeves ever so slightly.

BLONDE LACE

A group of young girls standing outside a badly built shopping mall. Somehow even if their dresses appear fashionable, something about them does not allow for them to rest well on these bodies.

⌘

The sleeves of that kind of shirt would have normally extended all the way down to her wrists, should her ams have been pointed downwards. Instead, she had the tailor finish off the sleeves somewhere mid-way on her forearms, leaving an impression that the sleeves that would normally have covered her arms were incomplete;

it was precisely this slight imperfection that made this shirt stand out.

⌘

 Later on in life, he would blame his parents for the drab clothes they dressed him in as a child, clothes that made him look later on like a dull, middle aged man.

⌘

She kept nothing on her person, on her slightly smelly, light-complectioned body after a long sweaty day. Her secrets, she used to say, and all that emotional baggage she had to carry lay heavily on the fabric of her oversized dresses or by now had gradually settled deep into the black corduroy jacket she wears in the winters.

⌘

Even though she was extraordinarily beautiful—she had a pretty face—the clothes she chose had very little to do with the image she presented of herself to the world. More so than anything else, they concealed certain realities she was hesitant to reveal. Although she appeared arrogant, she was desperate for a man's attention. She wanted him to look at her clothes when she walked by; they worked together and both looked forward everyday to the prospect of meeting each other in their clothes. She liked it when his top button was open so she could peer at the hair of his chest, or that one time when he came to work in his shorts, she couldn't take her eyes of his legs. Although she knew from the very outset that this long-drawn entanglement would come to nothing, she took pleasure in dressing up just for him and sending him photographs of the new dresses she bought for herself. This, she thought, she kept hidden from everyone else's gaze by wearing large tapestry-like capes she imagined concealed the whole affair.

⌘

For someone who was so driven to constantly look at herself in the mirror, she had a plain-clothes husband whom she constantly cheated on, if not physically, at least in her mind. It must have deeply disturbed her that he was always so shabbily dressed, and she never quite liked the shape of his head—she always feared for her progeny—although she would never have admitted this kind of thing to her well-dressed lovers with whom she would say that her husband was beyond such frills.

⌘

She wore her beautiful dresses only at home, for she did not want to attract the attention of passers-by outside; apart from her impractical fairytale house that looked like it had been put together by a dressmaker, she found that it was here, inside these ornate dresses she made her hiding places.

COUNTERFEIT TRADE MARKS

This three-piece suit broke all the rules of its own grammar, for its lines were crooked and the loops for the belt had come off and were now painfully stitched diagonally across the legs of the trousers; for the shirt buttons there were holes that only reminded one of buttons, rendering it difficult for the shirt to close. The wearer, as a result, would always end up walking with his arms tightly wrapped across his chest, forcing the two sides of his torso to close in on him.

⌘

Not much after wearing that jacket whose buttons criss-crossed, those bright pink pants accompanied with a yellow shirt, she had to remove these clothes to step into varying shades of black, as if suddenly entering a state of mourning on which this happiness of bright colored clothing was founded.

⌘

As a child I used to tear open the doors to rummage through my parents' wardrobe, imagining that I would learn more about them like this. Not only would I look at their clothes, I also remember caressing the fabric of my father's shirts and smelling the wool of my mother's shawls.

⌘

Her off-shoulder top—leaving one shoulder and bra-strap exposed—and her torn fragment-like jeans grazed against the grain of what was initially perceived as progress. It was as if by the use of a tiny pair of scissors we were altering history.

⌘

Her mother never let her buy new clothes. Every time she caught her walking in with a new skirt in her bag, she hung it in the cupboard and forbade her to ever wear it outside. She liked to dress her daughter every day with her own hands and in the clothes of her desire. She did this till the child was very old.

She always fancied having a fat boy, for her daughter was exceedingly thin. She would have fed him milk and put pieces of mutton in the blender for him to drink, before he even had teeth. As the clothes in the store would be too small for him, his mother would dress him up in clothes she would stitch herself.

HAIR OF THE CAMEL

This writer could not stop herself from borrowing clothes from her friends and began dressing up because she wanted passers-by to not notice her, but to look at her clothes, instead, so much so that she slowly lost interest in writing and spent most of her time thinking of what to wear.

⌘

Writing about fashion and literary writing is largely differentiated by the fact that literary writing gives birth and reality to life that did not exist before it was written while writing about fashion only refers to clothes that already exist in the world. Perhaps there could be a kind of writing that gives birth and life to a new kind of clothing, clothing that exists only in words, for at first it would be ostensibly difficult to liken the two, for one would comprise of verbs, subjects and predicates, and the other merely of fabric and color. However, there will come a point, perhaps with much effort, where these materials would bleed into one another, so much so that it would not be clear anymore as to whether we were really speaking of fabric or of grammar, of clothes or of the person wearing them.

CARRIAGE DRESS

It would have been expected to think that early explorers to the Arctic donned their garments as merely a means to keep warm and while they would have hardly dared dub their garb as fashion, they were, as a matter of fact, concerned not only about the function of their clothes but also what they looked like wearing them, even at the edges of the world, even almost at the brink of disappearing.

⌘

Because they already knew then they would always be wandering, they made sure to adorn their garments not only with glass—a means to deflect the gaze of those they would encounter along the way—but by intricate embroidery that chased along the bordering edges of all their clothes, a single undisturbed line woven into the fabric that not only spoke of their perpetual migration but also reminded them of where they came from. Who would have known that their past would soon begin to resemble the future.

⌘

The only way one could tell those twin girls apart was by how they were dressed.

⌘

She spent almost the whole day in a clothing store, lonely, until she finally bought a new skirt which she replaced with the one she had on before even leaving the store. She then went for a cup of coffee at a crowded café she would never have gone to were it not for her new skirt.

A PARTIAL LIST OF SNUGGLY BOOKS

G. ALBERT AURIER *Elsewhere and Other Stories*

S. HENRY BERTHOUD *Misanthropic Tales*

LÉON BLOY *The Desperate Man*

LÉON BLOY *The Tarantulas' Parlor and Other Unkind Tales*

ÉLÉMIR BOURGES *The Twilight of the Gods*

JAMES CHAMPAGNE *Harlem Smoke*

FÉLICIEN CHAMPSAUR *The Latin Orgy*

BRENDAN CONNELL *Clark*

BRENDAN CONNELL *Unofficial History of Pi Wei*

RAFAELA CONTRERAS *The Turquoise Ring and Other Stories*

ADOLFO COUVE *When I Think of My Missing Head*

QUENTIN S. CRISP *Aiaigasa*

LADY DILKE *The Outcast Spirit and Other Stories*

CATHERINE DOUSTEYSSIER-KHOZE
 The Beauty of the Death Cap

ÉDOUARD DUJARDIN *Hauntings*

BERIT ELLINGSEN *Now We Can See the Moon*

BERIT ELLINGSEN *Vessel and Solsvart*

ERCKMANN-CHATRIAN *A Malediction*

ENRIQUE GÓMEZ CARRILLO *Sentimental Stories*

EDMOND AND JULES DE GONCOURT *Manette Salomon*

REMY DE GOURMONT *From a Faraway Land*

GUIDO GOZZANO *Alcina and Other Stories*

EDWARD HERON-ALLEN *The Complete Shorter Fiction*

RHYS HUGHES *Cloud Farming in Wales*

J.-K. HUYSMANS *The Crowds of Lourdes*

J.-K. HUYSMANS *Knapsacks*

COLIN INSOLE *Valerie and Other Stories*

JUSTIN ISIS *Pleasant Tales II*

JUSTIN ISIS AND DANIEL CORRICK (editors)
 Drowning in Beauty: The Neo-Decadent Anthology

MARIE KRYSINSKA *The Path of Amour*
BERNARD LAZARE *The Mirror of Legends*
BERNARD LAZARE *The Torch-Bearers*
MAURICE LEVEL *The Shadow*
JEAN LORRAIN *Errant Vice*
JEAN LORRAIN *Fards and Poisons*
JEAN LORRAIN *Masks in the Tapestry*
JEAN LORRAIN *Nightmares of an Ether-Drinker*
ARTHUR MACHEN *N*
ARTHUR MACHEN *Ornaments in Jade*
CAMILLE MAUCLAIR *The Frail Soul and Other Stories*
CATULLE MENDÈS *Bluebirds*
CATULLE MENDÈS *For Reading in the Bath*
CATULLE MENDÈS *Mephistophela*
ÉPHRAÏM MIKHAËL *Halyartes and Other Poems in Prose*
LUIS DE MIRANDA *Who Killed the Poet?*
OCTAVE MIRBEAU *The Death of Balzac*
CHARLES MORICE *Babels, Balloons and Innocent Eyes*
DAMIAN MURPHY *Daughters of Apostasy*
DAMIAN MURPHY *The Star of Gnosia*
KRISTINE ONG MUSLIM *Butterfly Dream*
PHILOTHÉE O'NEDDY *The Enchanted Ring*
YARROW PAISLEY *Mendicant City*
URSULA PFLUG *Down From*
JEREMY REED *When a Girl Loves a Girl*
ADOLPHE RETTÉ *Misty Thule*
JEAN RICHEPIN *The Bull-Man and the Grasshopper*
DAVID RIX *A Blast of Hunters*
DAVID RIX *A Suite in Four Windows*
FREDERICK ROLFE (Baron Corvo) *Amico di Sandro*
FREDERICK ROLFE (Baron Corvo)
    An Ossuary of the North Lagoon and Other Stories

JASON ROLFE *An Archive of Human Nonsense*
MARCEL SCHWOB *The Assassins and Other Stories*
BRIAN STABLEFORD (editor)
  Decadence and Symbolism: A Showcase Anthology
BRIAN STABLEFORD (editor) *The Snuggly Satyricon*
BRIAN STABLEFORD *The Insubstantial Pageant*
BRIAN STABLEFORD *Spirits of the Vasty Deep*
BRIAN STABLEFORD *The Truths of Darkness*
COUNT ERIC STENBOCK *Love, Sleep & Dreams*
COUNT ERIC STENBOCK *Myrtle, Rue & Cypress*
COUNT ERIC STENBOCK *The Shadow of Death*
COUNT ERIC STENBOCK *Studies of Death*
MONTAGUE SUMMERS *Six Ghost Stories*
GILBERT-AUGUSTIN THIERRY
  Reincarnation and Redemption
DOUGLAS THOMPSON *The Fallen West*
TOADHOUSE *Gone Fishing with Samy Rosenstock*
TOADHOUSE *Living and Dying in a Mind Field*
RUGGERO VASARI *Raun*
JANE DE LA VAUDÈRE *The Demi-Sexes and The Androgynes*
JANE DE LA VAUDÈRE
  The Double Star and Other Occult Fantasies
JANE DE LA VAUDÈRE
  The Mystery of Kama and Brahma's Courtesans
JANE DE LA VAUDÈRE *The Priestesses of Mylitta*
JANE DE LA VAUDÈRE *Syta's Harem and Pharaoh's Lover*
AUGUSTE VILLIERS DE L'ISLE-ADAM *Isis*
RENÉE VIVIEN *Lilith's Legacy*
RENÉE VIVIEN *A Woman Appeared to Me*
TERESA WILMS MONTT *In the Stillness of Marble*
TERESA WILMS MONTT *Sentimental Doubts*
KAREL VAN DE WOESTIJNE *The Dying Peasant*